Goodbye, Charley

Also by Jane Buchanan

The Berry-Picking Man
Gratefully Yours
Hank's Story

Goodbye, Charley

Jane Buchanan

Farrar Straus Giroux
New York

*The author gratefully acknowledges
Melody Orr, secretary of the Simian
Society of America, for her critical
reading of the manuscript.*

Library of Congress Cataloging-in-Publication Data
Buchanan, Jane.
    Goodbye, Charley / Jane Buchanan.— 1st ed.
        p.   cm.
    Summary: In 1943, twelve-year-old Celie's father brings home a rhesus
monkey that helps Celie deal with all the difficulties that the war has brought
into her life in Gloucester, Massachusetts.
    ISBN 0-374-35020-5
    1. World War, 1939–1945—Massachusetts—Gloucester—Juvenile Fiction.
[1. World War, 1939–1945—United States—Fiction.   2. Rhesus monkey—
Fiction.   3. Monkeys—Fiction.   4. Family life—Massachusetts—Fiction.
5. Gloucester (Mass.)—History—20th century—Fiction.]   I. Title.

PZ7.B87714Go 2004
[Fic]—dc22

                                                          2003061054

For the Marshalls, here and gone.
And for Cheeta.

Author's Note

I grew up listening to tales of the monkey my grandfather brought home with him from work one day. Cheeta lived with my grandparents for many years, and the stories of his antics were recounted by my mother, my grandfather and grandmother, and my uncles, usually to laughter, but sometimes to tears.

And so I'd like to thank my grandfather for bringing Cheeta home, and my grandmother for the notes she saved, intending to write Cheeta's story herself someday. Thanks, too, to my uncle Stuffy for the stories he shared, and especially to my mother, who remembered the tears.

This story takes place in Gloucester, Massachusetts, but it also takes place in my memory and imagination. I hope those of you who know this city better than I will forgive any changes in geographic detail that may have been made to accommodate the story or my childhood memory.

Any work of historical fiction requires a fair amount of research. Thanks to Sarah Rasmussen, reference librarian at the Sawyer Free Library in Gloucester, and to Ellen Nelson, research librarian at the Cape Ann Historical Association, for help with Gloucester history. And thanks to Rick Nowell, chairman of the Archives Committee of the Boston & Maine Railroad Historical Society, for digging up the price of a ticket from Gloucester to Boston in 1943. Linda Rohr of Zoo New England helped with the description of the zoo in 1943 and tried to track down Cheeta's records. Petty Officer Edward Damico of the Naval Recruiting Office in Roslindale, Massachusetts, helped me locate the Boston recruiting office.

Ray Hamel of the Wisconsin Regional Primate Research Center alerted me to the changes in rhesus monkeys during puberty, and the center provided invaluable videotapes of the behavior of rhesus monkeys. Melody Orr, secretary of the Simian Society of America, also provided information about monkey development. Linda Eidell and Joyce Imel, interlibrary loan librarians at Meadville Public Library, filled my many requests for materials. I am indebted to these people.

My gratitude, also, to Sally Wilkins, Muriel Dubois, and Kathy Deady of the New Hampshire group, who heard it first and always believed.

Finally, this book could never have been completed without the infinite patience and gentle guidance of my editor, Beverly Reingold. Thank you.

Goodbye, Charley

1

Celie looked up at the gulls circling overhead and breathed deeply. There was nothing to compare to the rich, earthy smell of the salt-marsh flats, thick with the scent of fish and decay.

She wiggled her toes and felt the fine gray muck slide between them. Her mother wouldn't approve, she knew, of her going barefoot in the marsh. Ma worried about sharp shells and rusted fishhooks. But Celie loved the feel of the stuff on her feet. Besides, since rubber was rationed because of the war, the only boots she had were her brother Ben's, and they were so big the suction kept pulling them off.

Celie stabbed the pronged clamming shovel into the mud. Water bubbled up through small round holes, a sure sign that clams were there. She turned over the forkful and pawed through, quickly picking out the clams before they burrowed out of reach. Clamming was one of the things she loved most about summer in Gloucester, second only to eating the clams dipped in batter and fried in oil.

Celie picked up a particularly large clam and gazed at it admiringly. Its fat neck retracted into its shell, and she tossed it into one of the pails she had lined with seaweed to keep the clams moist. She wished she could show that monster to someone, but her best friend, Rita, had moved away right after school had ended, and now she had to go clamming alone. Now she did most everything alone. She'd never been much good at making friends, and these days her little brother, Andy, spent most of his time collecting junk for the Junior Commandos with his friend Rufus. Her older brother, Ben, who used to be okay, had turned into a big bully. Besides, who wanted to hang around with a bunch of boys? Not Celie!

Anyhow, it had been good clamming. She'd been at it since daybreak and had a couple of pails full. She would take them home so Ma could shuck them and fry them up for supper. Fat was hard to come by since the war. Ma always managed to find some for frying clams, though. It was, hands down, Celie's favorite meal. The only thing that could make it better was some fresh fried flounder dunked in ketchup. But today was Wednesday. Papa wouldn't be able to take her out in the boat until Saturday.

Celie swatted at the greenhead flies buzzing hungrily around her looking for blood. She pulled on Ben's boots and tucked the clamming fork under her arm. Her fingers were raw from the salt and sand, and when she picked up her pails the handles dug into her skin. She was hot and tired and hungry. Her back and shoulders ached. It had been a great morning. She carried the pails down to the shore and filled them with seawater to clean the clams, then headed for home.

Celie crossed the drawbridge and walked past the statue of the fisherman that stood at the entrance to the harbor. She couldn't avoid seeing the navy ships anchored there, gray and constant as barnacles, a reminder of the war her big brother was so eager to go off and fight in. She shook her head, flinging her long red braids back over her shoulders, and shifted the pails in her hands. At the same time, she stepped on a clamshell a gull had dropped on the sidewalk and nearly lost her balance. She kicked the shell hard, and it went skittering away with a clatter, her boot along with it. "Shoot," she said. She put down the pails and pulled the boot back on.

By the time she got home, Celie felt as though her arms had stretched five inches from the weight of the pails. She leaned the clamming fork against the house and pushed open the front door with her foot.

Ma was standing at the kitchen sink up to her elbows in suds. Her long hair was coiled like a pinwheel at the back of her neck. "Take off those boots before you go another step," she said sternly. Then she smiled. "Good clamming?"

"Great," said Celie, kicking off her boots and plunking the pails down on the counter.

Ma admired the clams and put a cold meat-loaf sandwich on the table. "Wash up and eat some lunch," she said. "And scrub those feet! I don't suppose you were clamming barefoot again." It was more of a statement than a question.

Celie went to the bathroom and washed her feet one at a time under the tap in the sink. She splashed cold water on her flaming cheeks. Her braids flopped over her shoulders into the running water. She squeezed them out and popped the end of one into her mouth. It tasted salty from the damp ocean air at the marsh. She dried her feet on the clean white towel, then hung it back on the towel bar with the used side down so Ma wouldn't notice the smudges of marsh mud.

Celie sat at the table and spit out the braid to make room for a large bite of her sandwich.

"Papa called," Ma said. "Something about a surprise." Ma didn't look too thrilled. She always said Papa's surprises meant more work for her.

"Did he say what kind of surprise?" Celie asked. Unlike Ma, she usually liked her father's surprises. "Animal or mineral?"

Ma shrugged. "Didn't say," she said.

Celie took another bite of her sandwich. It wasn't bad considering that the meat loaf was more oatmeal than meat. It was the summer of 1943. The country had been at war for a year and a half, and meat was only one of the things that were scarce. Celie sometimes thought it would be faster to list what hadn't been rationed since the Japanese bombed Pearl Harbor on December 7, 1941, and President Roosevelt talked on the radio about a day that would live in infamy. She couldn't remember the last time she'd had a butter-and-sugar sandwich or worn a new pair of shoes. Not that she cared much for shoes, but sometimes they were necessary and the less they pinched her toes, the better.

She finished her sandwich and washed it down with a glass of milk. Then she went up to her room and changed into dry clothes—a yellow blouse and a pair of her brother's hand-me-down dungarees rolled to her ankles and cinched around her waist with a worn leather belt. She slipped her sneakers on over her bare feet and, grabbing her baseball and mitt, ran back down the stairs.

"I'm going to the park," she said. "See if there's a game."

"I was hoping you'd help me in the garden," Ma said. "And the dandelions out front need to be dug."

"When I get back," Celie said. "I promise."

"Uh-huh," said Ma. She'd heard that before. "Dinner's at five." Celie was nearly at the door when Ma added, "Did you hang your wet things to dry?"

"Mmm," Celie said, hoping Ma would take the noncommittal grunt as a yes, which she told herself was not technically a lie.

The damp chill of the early morning had long burned off and been replaced by the hot, humid air of a summer afternoon. As Celie started out the door, Ma yelled after her, "Go down to the beach and see if Andy's there! See if he wants to play."

"Okay!" Celie called back, tearing down the gravel driveway as the screen door slapped shut behind her and nearly running smack into old Mrs. Bentley from next door. "Hey, Mrs. B.," Celie said, forcing a smile to her lips.

Mrs. Bentley could teach the crabs down at the marsh a thing or two, Celie always thought. She was about as hard and spindly as a crab, too. She spent so much time with her lips pursed that she had permanent wrinkles all around her mouth. She was pursing them now.

"Hay is for horses," she said.

Celie gritted her teeth. Mrs. Bentley had lived next door forever. She'd had a husband once, but that was before Celie was born. He'd died years ago, when his boat went down in a storm. As long as Celie had known her, Mrs. Bentley had been old and crabby and alone. And she seemed to like it that way. Before Ben got old enough, Mrs. Bentley had been their baby-sitter. These days, though, when Ben wasn't around, Ma trusted Celie to watch Andy. She was twelve and three quarters, plenty old enough to baby-sit a six-year-old.

"I'm going to the beach," Celie said, because she couldn't think of anything else to say that wouldn't cause Mrs. Bentley to make disapproving comments, and dashed off before the old sourpuss had time to notice the baseball mitt tucked under her arm. Mrs. Bentley definitely didn't approve of girls playing baseball.

The beach was across the street and over the hill. Celie always took the shortcut through the cemetery. A couple of new graves had appeared since the war started. Small, faded American flags fluttered in the summer breeze.

At the bottom of the hill, near the beach, was a little shop that served sandwiches and ice cream. Ice cream was hard to come by these days, what with sugar and dairy rationing, but you could still get it, though not as much as you might like, and not in all your favorite flavors. It didn't make sense to Celie. How come she couldn't have a butter-and-sugar sandwich, but anyone with a nickel could go to the Cupboard and buy a cone? "Has to do with morale on the home front," Papa had said. "Have to keep folks happy at home so they'll keep supporting the war effort, and everyone knows that ice cream is essential for morale." He'd tugged Celie's braid and grinned.

At the beach a few families had spread out their blankets like patchwork. There was no sign of Andy. At least she could tell Ma she'd looked for him.

She started toward the park. Maybe there was already a game going. She ran into Andy and Rufus making their way up the sidewalk, hauling a rusty red wagon heaped with junk.

"How's it going?" she asked them. Like most of the kids in America nowadays, Andy and Rufus went around collecting things for the war effort: bacon grease, tin cans, worn-out pots and pans, ladies' nylon stockings, even old rags. It was hard to believe the government could win a war with all that old junk, but Papa had said they made bombs from the bacon fat and parachutes from the nylon. She didn't know what else they did with the stuff, but she figured Andy and Rufus had gathered tons of it over the last year.

"Okay," said Andy, pulling up the wagon so Celie could see.

"Great!" said Celie, pretending to admire the jumble of stuff. It looked like a mess to her, and the smell of rancid bacon grease nearly made her gag. "I'm going down to the ball field," she said, backing away. "Wanna come?"

"Nah," said Andy. "Ben's there. He told us to scram."

Celie reached out and tousled Andy's hair. "Don't mind Ben," she said. "He's too big for his britches, that's all."

It was true. Ben had become an air-raid warden when the war had started, and he thought he was the cat's meow. Ma just shook her head when the sirens went off and Ben came in ordering the family under the kitchen table while he searched the attic for incendiary bombs. Celie wasn't sure how they were supposed to have gotten there, but it was part of the drill. Ben never let them skip it. Celie would climb under the table and hold her hands over her ears. She hated these drills. They were like dark clouds hanging over their lives, reminding them that the Germans could attack for real any minute, dropping bombs on their houses and destroying everything. Drills were the only times she wished they didn't live on the coast, where they'd be the first targets in an attack. It didn't help that people had started to think maybe Massachusetts wouldn't get attacked by the Germans; Celie knew that U-boats had sunk plenty of ships along the East Coast. There was no telling when the Germans might decide to invade. So she still got a cold chill when she heard that siren go off.

But not Ma. "I have too much to do to be hiding under the kitchen table, Benjamin Marsh," Ma would say, wiping her hands on her apron. "As if a table is going to save us from a German bomb." That didn't make Celie feel any better. She liked to think that even if the house was demolished, the kitchen table would protect them. She knew, if she thought about it, that it didn't make much sense, but she needed to believe it. She wished Ma believed it, too. Eventually Ma would shake her head and get down on her hands and knees and climb under the table with the rest of them. "Lord," she'd say, looking up at the underside of the table as though heaven were made of maple boards and smeared with Andy's greasy fingerprints, "if this war doesn't kill us, these air-raid drills will!"

Ben said Ma was being unpatriotic when she talked like that. He said it was her duty as an American to take these things seriously, just as it was her duty to draw her blackout curtains every night to keep the light from showing.

"As if the Germans don't know we're here," Ma would say, tugging the heavy black curtains across the windows.

Celie worried sometimes that Ma would get into trouble for talking that way. She wished her mother would be more careful. There was a war on, after all. There were billboards and signs everywhere to remind you that the enemy was listening. It made Celie nervous.

Down at the ball field, the guys were well into a game. No chance for Celie to play now. She sat on the bench behind home plate, next to Billy Jessup, who was there in his wheelchair. His sister, Ina, always brought him over to watch the games.

"Hey," Celie said as she brushed off the bench and sat down. Billy and Ina both smiled, but they kept their eyes on the game. Celie tried not to look at Billy's legs—or rather where his legs had been. She hated to think about what it must have been like losing them the way he did in the war. He was lucky to be alive, people said. She wondered if he felt lucky. She watched the game, tossing her ball back and forth from her hand to her glove. She wished she had some-one to play catch with, but Ina didn't play ball, and Billy couldn't unless you threw the ball right to him.

The game was close. One team was Portuguese boys from up on Portagee Hill. The other was mostly what Papa called WASPs—like them, white Anglo-Saxon Protestants. The Portagee Hill team was winning, and Ben looked glum. He hated to lose, but he especially hated to lose to the Portagees. That had gotten worse since the war started. There was talk that the Portagees weren't real Americans and couldn't be trusted. People said some of the Portuguese fishermen who went out looking for U-boats were really passing on classified information. Celie didn't believe that, though, and she didn't see how hating people for being Por-tuguese was any different from hating people for being Jew-ish, and wasn't that one of the things we were over there fighting about?

Celie watched and cheered Ben's team on. She cheered the Portagee Hill team, too. Jimmy DaSilva was playing third base. He tipped his chin in Celie's direction and winked. Celie looked down at her mitt and tossed her ball back and forth. Jimmy was what Celie's ma called a real charmer. Celie'd known him since she was a little kid. He and Ben had been friends until Ben got in with a crowd that didn't have much use for the Portuguese—and Jimmy showed that he wasn't crazy about Ben's girlfriend, who was part of that crowd. But Jimmy had always been nice to Celie, like a big brother—the big brother that Ben wasn't much anymore. Jimmy looked out for her. He was eighteen and would have been off fighting if he hadn't lost the last two fingers of his throwing hand in a fishing accident. He could still throw a baseball, though. He'd given Celie plenty of pointers on pitching. Jimmy was a lobsterman. He didn't play ball much these days, but sometimes, when the younger guys needed a ninth man, he'd fill in if he wasn't too busy.

In the end, Ben's team lost on a hard liner to third. Ben went off with friends, and Jimmy headed down to the docks. Ina and Billy Jessup said goodbye and left. Celie sat slumped on the bench, her chin propped in her glove hand.

2

Celie was about to get up and start home when she noticed her father walking down the street. She hadn't realized it was so late. From the pucker of his lips, she could tell he was whistling. He was carrying a big square box. The surprise. She'd forgotten all about it.

"Papa!" Celie called. She stood up on the bench and waved both her arms over her head. Her father stopped whistling and broke into a broad grin. Ma always said he looked like a little boy when he did that. Sometimes she said he acted like one, too. Celie wondered whether it was a compliment when Ma told her, "You're just like your father." Doing things without thinking about the consequences was probably what she meant.

"What's in the box?" Celie asked when he finally reached her. "Ma said you were bringing a surprise. Can I see it?" She grabbed on to his forearm. Papa's shirtsleeve was rolled up and his arm, damp with sweat, was solid as a tree trunk.

"Hey, Smudge," Papa said, raising the box up higher. He called her Smudge because she was so small when she was born. No more than a smudge, he always said. She still was a shrimp, compared to other kids her age.

Celie thought she heard the box squawk. "Animal!" she squealed, letting go of Papa's arm and trying to peek into the box through one of the small holes punched in its side.

He handed her a paper package, which had been balanced on top. She could tell by the heavy dampness that it was fish. "Flounder," he said. "Fresh from the harbor. And what's in the box is a present from Mickey. He's home on leave." Before the war Mickey had worked in the shop with Papa. Now he was in the merchant marines. Papa worked a Linotype machine at the newspaper, putting lead letters together in wooden galleys to print words on paper. Celie always thought it must be hard to write everything backward so it would print out frontward the way it did.

Celie moved to grab the box, but Papa swung it away and out of reach.

"Wait till we get home," he said, laughing again.

He slipped past her and broke into a trot as he headed across the park toward home. The box squawked again and, sticking out of a hole in the corner, Celie was sure she saw a small brown finger.

When they reached the front door, Papa said, "Go in and tell Ma to close her eyes and come here."

Celie looked sideways at him. "Are you sure that's a good idea, Papa?" she said.

"Go on." The way Papa was grinning, you'd think he was a genie about to grant all their wishes. He set the box on the stoop. Celie opened the door and went in. Ma was in the summer kitchen putting laundry through the wringer.

"Hey, Ma," Celie said.

Ma looked up. "Hmm?" she said.

"Papa's home." Celie was so excited she could hardly keep from jumping up and down.

"Oh?" Ma eyed her suspiciously.

The summer kitchen was off the regular kitchen. It had a concrete floor and walls with shelves where Ma stacked all the food she canned from her Victory Garden. There was an old gas stove and two big slate sinks. The porcelain wringer-washer squatted on four legs in one corner. Clotheslines, where Ma hung laundry to dry on rainy days, crisscrossed the ceiling.

"He wants you to close your eyes and go to the front door."

"I'll go to the door," Ma said, "but I won't close my eyes. You know how I feel about surprises."

Celie nodded. "I know," she said.

Ma wiped her hands on her apron and started toward the door with Celie at her heels.

"It has brown fingers," Celie said, though she knew Papa wouldn't want her telling. "And it squawks."

"Oh Lord," said Ma.

When they got to the door, Ma stopped short and put her hand up to her mouth. Celie almost walked right into her.

"What?" Celie asked, straining to see past Ma, who was blocking her view. "What is it?" She peeked around Ma to see what had shocked her so.

"Oh," Celie said. It was more of a gasp than a word. Sitting on Papa's shoulder was a monkey. Hunched the way it was, it looked about the size of a raccoon or a large brown cat.

Papa was beaming. "It's a monkey," he said. As if they couldn't tell. "Mickey gave him to me," he went on. "Remember I said Mickey was coming home on leave? Thought the kids might like a pet." Ma still had her hand over her mouth, so Papa just kept on talking. "Mickey says he's a couple years old. Not a baby or anything. Brought him all the way from India."

Ma finally found her voice. "India Schmindia," she said. "What in heaven's name"—she was measuring each word carefully—"are we going to do with a monkey? What were you thinking, George? What was Mickey thinking?" She was picking up speed now. "I don't have enough to do around here without looking after a monkey?" And volume. "There's a war on, George. There are shortages of everything. I don't know what monkeys eat, but whatever it is, I'm sure we don't have ration stamps for it!"

But Celie was barely listening. She was watching the monkey. He was leaning forward and looking down at Ma with his quick brown eyes. His mouth was open and he was making mewing sounds. He was flicking his ears back and forth and his eyebrows were raised in a look of surprise. For Celie, it was love at first sight. "Aw, Ma," she said, "I'll take care of him. You won't have to do a thing."

"Uh-huh," said Ma. "I've heard that before."

Celie looked down at her feet and wiggled her toes

through the holes in her sneakers. This wasn't the first time Papa had brought home an animal out of the blue. There had been dogs, stray cats, even a goat. And there was the brief period when they'd shared the bathtub with a baby alligator. There had been promises then, too. But this time it was different. This time she meant it.

"I'm almost thirteen years old," Celie said, using the argument Ma always used on her—You're practically a teenager, you should know better! "Practically a teenager. I guess I can take care of a little monkey."

Ma still looked skeptical.

"Mickey says he'll eat about anything," Papa said. "Likes fruit, though, and vegetables. Meat, too, even, I guess."

"Mmm," said Ma. Her lips were pressed tightly together.

Papa swung the monkey down from his shoulder and handed him to Celie. "Here," he said. "Why don't you take him outside while Ma and I talk." He gave Celie a wink.

"I saw that, George," Ma said as Celie headed out the door. "Don't think you can sweet-talk me!"

The monkey was warm and soft, and lighter than she expected. He smelled like a mixture of the dank must of the basement after a rain and the sourness of sweat. He reached up and put his arms around Celie's neck. His leathery hands, which looked like a small child's except the fingers were longer, were cool and moist. She looked into his eyes, brown as chocolate Tootsie Pops, and grinned. For the first time in weeks, she felt as though she had a true soul mate. She had to keep him; she just had to.

Celie carried the monkey out the back door and into the

yard. He was wearing a wide leather belt that buckled in front and had a long chain attached to a metal ring on the back. Celie held the chain tight. When they got outside, she put the monkey down, and he scampered right over to the stone wall that separated their yard from Mrs. Bentley's. On all fours, he looked a bit like a lion the way he rolled his shoulders from side to side. His back legs were slightly longer than his arms, so his rear end stuck up and his tail stood tall and straight as a flagpole. He jumped up onto the wall and squatted there with his arm resting on his knee.

Celie laughed. She sat down on the wall next to him and lifted him onto her lap. Through the screen door she could hear her parents' voices.

"I just wish you would talk to me before you do things like this," Ma said.

"Come on, Lizzy," Papa said, and Celie could picture him smiling, putting his hands on Ma's waist, looking into her eyes the way Celie imagined he must have when the two of them were courting. A charmer, like Jimmy. "It's just a little monkey. What harm could it do?"

"What harm?" Ma said. She'd have stepped away, shaking Papa's hands off, not buying his sweet talk. "You've heard the expression 'monkey business'?"

Celie looked at the monkey sitting hunched up on her lap. "You're not going to be a troublemaker, are you?"

As though to answer her question, the monkey jumped to his feet and scrambled up the chestnut tree next to the wall, pulling his leash right out of her hand.

"Hey!" she said, shaking her hand to ease the sting of the

chain's scraping through it. "Come back here!" She looked at her fingers. They were pink but not bleeding.

The leaves on the tree were thick, but she could still see the tree house Ben and Papa had built one summer when Ben was little. It wasn't much of a house, really, just a platform set into the crook of some branches. Ben had gotten too old for it, but Celie loved to climb up there on long summer days and read.

When the monkey reached the platform, he stopped and sat down, dangling his legs off the side. After a minute he got up and started to explore. Celie lost sight of him through the branches. She was about to climb up after him when she heard a rustling in the leaves and then a shriek.

Mrs. Bentley was walking up the sidewalk. Her hat was askew on her head, making her look a bit tipsy. A shiny brown chestnut was rolling along the concrete, coming to a stop in the grass.

Oh jeepers, Celie thought, he must have found my stash. She and Rita always kept a basket of chestnuts in the tree house for bombarding Ben and his pals. At least they used to, before Rita decided she'd rather flirt with boys than pelt them with horse chestnuts. Looking at Mrs. Bentley now, Celie was glad she had peeled off all the chestnuts' prickly outsides last fall.

"What do you mean by throwing chestnuts at me, young lady?" Mrs. Bentley asked crossly. "I will speak to your mother about this." Her hand shook as she stuck out the black umbrella she used as a cane and pointed it at Celie.

"Oh, Mrs. B.," Celie said, crossing her fingers behind her back and hoping the monkey knew enough to keep his mouth shut, "I'm really sorry. I was practicing my pitching and I guess it got away from me."

Mrs. Bentley frowned. "Maybe you should put your efforts into more ladylike endeavors." She didn't think girls should do anything besides cook and sew and clean. But she seemed satisfied that Celie was sorry.

"You just be careful, miss," she said, and walked on by, clacking her umbrella tip on the sidewalk as she went.

"You just be careful, miss," Celie mimicked. Then to the monkey she said, "You owe me one, pal!"

The monkey squawked something that sounded like a laugh and Celie felt the sting of a chestnut connecting with her scalp. "Hey!" she cried. She looked up. The monkey was standing, holding the nearest branch with both hands and shaking it with all his might, squawking loudly. It was a little scary. With his mouth open that way, Celie could see his canine teeth, like little daggers in his mouth. She was about to run for her father when the monkey stopped suddenly and sat back on his perch in the tree.

Just then, Papa came out of the house. "Where's the monkey?" he asked, looking around the yard.

Celie pointed to the tree house.

Her father looked up. "How'd he get up there?"

"I thought he needed some exercise," Celie said, crossing her fingers behind her back. No need to let Papa know he'd gotten away from her. "So what'd Ma say?"

"She said we can keep him for now, see how it goes."

Celie grinned. "I knew she wouldn't be able to send him away."

"Not so fast," Papa said. "He's still on probation, so he'd better behave."

"He will," said Celie. She'd make sure of that.

In the tree the monkey squawked again, and Celie turned to climb up and get him. "He's not going to be any trouble, Papa," she said. "I swear. I'll take good care of him. Ma won't even know he's here."

But before Celie could get one sneaker on the tree house ladder, there was another rustling in the leaves.

"Ow!" Papa hollered. "What the heck?" He looked up into the tree, then he looked at Celie. A shiny brown chestnut was rolling on the ground at his feet.

Celie barely stifled a laugh.

Papa rubbed his scalp. "Maybe you should find a new hiding place for those chestnuts," he said. "If he keeps this up, it's gonna be 'Goodbye, Charley.' "

Goodbye, Charley, Celie thought. Like the song she used to play on the piano before Ma finally let her quit her lessons.

"Charley who?" It was Ben. Andy was right behind him, towing his wagon full of junk. Ma said the two of them had clocks in their stomachs that told them when it was suppertime.

Ben was carrying his baseball mitt under his arm. His white undershirt was torn and smeared with fish blood from his morning down at the docks, where he worked part time in the summer. His baseball cap was pushed up on his head so his cowlick stuck straight up in front. Andy looked like a miniature version of his big brother, except his hair was curlier and he had a couple of teeth missing in front.

"Charley nobody," Celie said. "But, come to think of it, that's a good name, Charley."

"For who?" Ben was beginning to look annoyed. What else was new?

"For our new pet," she said. She turned and was about to start up the tree when Ben shouted.

"Ow! Hey, what was that?" He looked up, trying to see what had hit him. "What the—?"

"A monkey! A real live monkey!" cried Andy.

Celie laughed. "Good shot, fella!" she yelled. "Bull's-eye!"

"Maybe you should get him out of there," Papa said, smiling.

"Get who out of where?" Ben asked. "What's going on here?"

"Papa brought us a surprise," Celie said as she climbed up to the tree house. The monkey moved to the edge of the platform and watched her. "Come on, boy." She spoke softly and moved slowly. The last thing she wanted to do was send him scurrying farther up the tree. She reached out her arms and picked him up. "Charley," she said. "What do you think, fella? You like the name Charley?"

The monkey chuckled and Celie took that as a sign of

agreement. She picked him up and carried him back down the tree.

Andy dropped the handle of his wagon and ran over for a better look. "Can I hold him?"

Charley clung to Celie's shirt and looked wide-eyed at Andy, who was hopping with excitement.

"Whoa, Tarzan," Papa said. "I think you're scaring him."

"You have to be quiet," Celie said, holding a finger to her lips. "Until he gets to know you."

"Yeah," said Ben, rubbing his head, "wouldn't want to scare the poor little thing. Cripes." He shook his head in disgust and Papa shot him a warning look.

Andy tiptoed forward. "Can I hold him?" he whispered.

"Not yet," Celie said. "Why don't you say hello first." She bent down so Andy could get a better look. "Charley, meet Andy."

"Hello, Charley," Andy whispered. Charley squawked and Andy jumped back with a giggle.

"Aw, cripes," Ben said again. "I can't wait until I can join the navy and get out of this zoo."

That was his response to most everything these days. Sometimes Celie thought she could hardly wait, either. But then she thought about what could happen to him over there, and she knew she didn't mean that. She didn't want him to come back in a wheelchair, or worse, be one more waving flag in the cemetery. Sure he was a pain, but he was her brother. And she could still remember when they used to do everything together. Maybe, when the war was over, it would be like that again.

"Well now," said Papa, who didn't like to hear talk about Ben enlisting, mostly because he knew it upset Ma, "I guess we'd all better wash up and get ready for supper. Andy, you put your collections in the shed and, Celie, you tie Charley here up." He felt his head where the chestnut had hit him and added, "Preferably where he can't reach the tree house."

3

Inside, the kitchen was rich with the smell of hot fat, clams, and frying fish. It was going to be a feast. Celie's mouth watered.

"Wash your hands," Ma ordered. Celie and Andy went dutifully to the sink to clean up.

"Did you see Charley, Ma?" Andy said.

"Charley?" Ma said.

"The monkey," said Andy. "Celie said his name is Charley."

"Oh, the monkey," said Ma. "We've named him already, have we?" She raised an eyebrow at Celie. "Yes, Andrew, I saw him. Now, you help Celie set the table."

Celie got plates and glasses out of the cupboard and put them on the table. Andy laid forks and freshly laundered napkins at each place. Papa and Ben were in the living room listening to the war news on the radio. Something about the marines in New Georgia fighting to take the Solomon Islands from the Japanese. Celie didn't like to think about the fighting, and she was grateful when Ma called, "All right, you two, turn off that noise and come eat."

"It's not noise, Ma," Ben said. "It's the news. It's important."

"So is supper," said Ma.

"Ma, our country is at war. It's your patriotic duty—"

"Don't talk to me about duty, young man," Ma snapped, and Papa fired off a look that told him to drop it.

To Celie's surprise, he did. They all sat there awkwardly for a while, with nobody talking at all, not even Andy. Ma was still upset about the monkey, Celie figured; otherwise she wouldn't have jumped all over Ben like that. But she understood how Ma could get tired of Ben preaching to her about duty. She did, too.

Celie piled a heap of clams and fish onto her plate, along with a dollop of tartar sauce and a pool of ketchup, and dug in. The clams were so tender they nearly melted on her tongue. "Mmm," she said, breaking the silence finally. "They're delicious, Ma."

"You've done it again, Liz," Papa said.

"Flattery will get you nowhere," Ma said. "Besides, Celie did the hard part. All I did was cook them."

"Well," said Papa, "since the rest of you did all the hard work, Ben and I will clean up. Won't we, Ben?"

Ben glowered.

"I think I can manage my own kitchen," Ma said. "Besides, I always end up a glass or two short when you do the dishes, and there are enough shortages around here these days."

Papa winked at Celie. "Yes, ma'am," he said. He piled his

own plate high. "So." He looked at Ben. "How was the game today?"

"They lost," Celie said.

Ben glared at her. "To the Portagees," he said. Ma shot him a disapproving glance, but Ben didn't look in her direction. Celie would have bet he felt Ma's eyes on him, though. Like a blowtorch. "If that Jimmy DaSilva hadn't been playing, we would have won," he went on, still ignoring Ma's fiery eyes. "I made a great play, Pop," he said. "You shoulda seen me. Just like Joltin' Joe."

"Oh, Joe DiMaggio," Celie said. "You and your New York Yankees. Everyone else in Massachusetts roots for the Boston Red Sox, or at least the Boston Braves. But not you."

"It doesn't much matter this year anyway," Papa said.

It was true. Since the war started, the good players on all the teams had joined up. The clubs were signing guys who couldn't get into the service because they were too old or they had only one arm or something. Celie couldn't wait for the war to be over so Ted Williams could get back into left field at Fenway Park, where he belonged. In the meantime, she hoped a girls' team would start up in Boston, like the All-American Girls Professional Baseball League that had formed in the Midwest that summer. She was about to say so, when she heard a loud holler from outside and a dog barking.

"Oh, no!" Celie yelled. "Wolfred!" She jumped up and ran to the back door.

There was the Nelsons' Saint Bernard barking his head

off. Charley was jumping up and down on the picnic table yelling, "Waaa! Waaa!"

The Nelsons were the Marshes' other next-door neighbors. Their dog was always straying into the Marshes' yard and getting into their garbage. Now he was after Charley.

When he saw Celie, Charley stood up and waved his hands as though to say, Come here! Save me! She ran to the table, and he scrambled up into her arms. Celie could feel his heart pounding, and he was trembling all over.

Finally Mr. Nelson came running into the yard. "What the deuce?" he said when he saw the monkey. Then he just stood there shaking his head while Wolfred snarled and barked.

After a few comments about the Marshes' pets, he took Wolfred by the collar and started home. "You just make sure you keep that thing tied up, George," he called back. "That darned goat of yours ate the Christmas wreaths off every door on the street."

Celie had a time trying to calm Charley down. He was clinging to her, his eyes wide and his mouth open, panting.

"Well," said Ma, looking almost sorry for him, "I guess you'd better bring him into the house while we finish eating. Then we can find a place for him to sleep. We can't very well leave him out here alone with Wolfred prowling the neighborhood."

Ma looked at the monkey, then she looked at Papa. "He is housebroken, isn't he?"

"Well," said Papa, giving Celie a wink, "we'll find out."

After supper everyone went out on the porch while Ma cleaned up. Charley examined all the corners, then climbed onto Celie's lap and sat quietly looking around.

"So, where'd you get the stupid thing anyway?" Ben asked.

"He's probably smarter than you," Celie said. Then she added, "Mickey down at the paper brought him back from India."

"That's right," Papa said. "Mickey joined the merchant marines a while ago. He just got back to the States and he came into the shop with this box. 'Hey, George,' he says, 'I brought you a present.' You could have knocked me over with a feather when I opened that box."

"Where's India?" Andy asked.

"Far away," Papa said, lifting Andy onto his lap. "All the way across the ocean."

"Wow," said Andy. His eyes shone as he looked at the monkey in Celie's lap.

It was dusk and the mosquitoes were beginning to swarm. In the yard, Celie could see fireflies flickering. Bats and barn swallows were starting their evening hunts to the rhythmic gonging of the bell buoys in the harbor. It was hard to believe, at times like this, that there was a war going on.

"Who ever heard of a monkey named Charley?" Ben asked.

"It's a nice name," said Celie. "What's it to you? You just said he was stupid."

"Yeah," said Ben. "Stupid Monkey. That's a good name."

"Benjamin." Papa sounded threatening again.

"Aw, who cares," Ben said. He got up and stomped inside. "Stupid monkey."

The screen door slammed shut behind him and the monkey jumped, startled. All of a sudden, Celie's lap felt warmer than before, and wetter.

"Hey, Papa," she said, "I think we just found out if he's housebroken."

★

"He was excited, that's all," Celie said when her mother saw her wet pants. "It's a new place. He didn't know where else to go."

"Uh-huh," said Ma. She took the monkey and handed Celie a clean towel. "You go take a bath while I find a place for the beast to sleep."

"He's not a beast," Celie said. "And besides, why can't he sleep with me?"

"Not likely," said Ma. "Clothes I can wash; a mattress is more difficult." She pursed her lips and put her hands on her hips. "There's an old grocery crate in the cellar," she said, "and there might be a few rags around that we haven't given to the war effort." She sighed. "I guess we can put him out in the summer kitchen. He can't do much damage there."

Charley was already asleep when Celie came down from her bath. He slept sitting up, crouching really, in the corner of the crate with his chin tucked into his chest. He looked small and helpless. She hoped he wouldn't get lonely out there.

She went into the living room and sat on the sofa across from the radio. *The Lone Ranger* had already started. It came on right after *I Love a Mystery*, her favorite show, but she'd already missed that. Ma had tucked Andy in and was knitting. Papa was snoring in his chair. Ben was staring intently at the radio, his eyebrows drawn together and his mouth turned down in a frown. Who knew what was going on in his head anymore, Celie thought.

She picked up the olive green sock she was making for the soldiers and began knitting. Ma was working on an olive green sweater. It was amazing that with all the shortages, there always seemed to be enough olive green yarn to knit more socks and sweaters.

Celie had been on the same sock forever. She wasn't much of a knitter anyway, and she got distracted by the stories they were listening to. She'd stare at the face of the big wooden radio and imagine Tonto and the Lone Ranger riding round the Wild West.

The radio was about as tall as Andy and had curlicues and swirls carved into the wood. It reminded Celie of a cathedral, like the ones in Germany and France that she'd seen pictures of in *Life* magazine. Papa said that with the bombing, there might not be many of those left standing after the war. It seemed a shame. For hundreds of years they'd been there, and then boom, rubble. It was scary how fast things could change.

Celie tried to concentrate on *The Lone Ranger* and keep

from dropping any stitches, but somehow she couldn't manage to keep her eyes open.

After she'd started awake for the third time, Ma said, "Celie, why don't you head on up to bed?"

"But Ma—" Celie began.

"No *buts*, young lady. Up you go."

"Yes, ma'am." Celie put her knitting back in the canvas bag that sat by the chair, kissed her parents good night, and went upstairs.

"You, too, Ben," Ma said, and in a few minutes she heard Ben clomping up the stairs. Celie couldn't remember the last time Ma had sent Ben to bed. And he hadn't even argued.

Celie's bedroom was above the living room, and after she went to bed she could hear her parents talking downstairs. Ma must have turned down the radio because their voices came through loud and clear.

"Everything is just getting to be too much," Ma said. "The war; rationing; worrying all the time that the Germans are going to attack. Ben will be eighteen in another year. He can't wait to go off and get into the fighting. And what if it goes on long enough that they start drafting older men?" There was a pause, and it sounded as though Ma was crying.

Celie lay in bed rigid as a post. A tingle of fear ran down her spine and into her toes, which she curled tightly to make the feeling go away. Ma was scared. That meant Celie was right to be frightened.

"It'll be all right, Liz," Papa said, but Ma wouldn't believe him, Celie knew. When you're scared, having someone tell you it's going to be all right doesn't help. How did Papa know? He couldn't predict the future. He didn't know how the war was going to end. "I'm sure they can't draft me with this bad ear of mine," he said.

Celie always forgot about Papa's bad ear. The doctor said it had been caused by the noisy presses at the shop, and Celie could believe it. The one time she was down in the pressroom, there was such a racket that she couldn't hear right for an hour afterward. She couldn't imagine listening to it all day. But just talking to him, you'd never think Papa had trouble hearing. Ma liked to say he heard fine when he wanted to; it was only when she asked him to do things that he suddenly went deaf.

"I just feel so helpless," Ma said. "I have to do something besides sit here and knit these foolish sweaters." The way she said it made Celie wonder if Ma already had a plan. She didn't want to think about that.

Her parents stopped talking then, and somebody turned up the radio. *The Lone Ranger* was over and the war news was on. More about the Solomon Islands.

Celie lay in bed thinking about Charley, and about Ma. To Celie, having a pet to keep you company made things seem a little less scary. When she was little, she could hug her doll. But she was too old for dolls now, and besides, she'd given hers to the rubber collection drive. The doll had probably been melted down long ago and made into Jeep tires. At least she'd had Rita then. Now she had no one—not even Ben. She needed Charley. She didn't see why he was worse than any other pet Papa had ever brought home. She thought he was better. Goats weren't very cuddly, and cats were so uppity. And you certainly wouldn't want to have an alligator in your bed. She'd just make sure Charley stayed out of Ma's hair, that's all. It would be fine.

4

Charley was already awake when Celie went downstairs the next morning. He scampered over and raised his arms to be picked up, the way Andy used to do when he was little. Celie swung him onto her hip and gave him the last of Ma's precious bananas from the bowl on the table. Ma frowned as he peeled the banana, took a couple of bites, and shoved the rest into his cheek pouch for later. His cheek bulged out, just like a chipmunk's. Then he pushed his shoulder up against his cheek and squeezed the banana into his mouth a bit at a time, as though it were toothpaste in a tube. Celie laughed. "Silly boy," she said.

Ma had made eggs and fried Spam for breakfast. Celie ate what she could and slipped what was left to Charley.

"All right, that's enough," Ma said when she caught her. Ma sounded tired, and Celie remembered her words last night—the last thing I need is a monkey. "Get that animal out of my kitchen. I have work to do."

Celie lifted Charley onto her shoulder and went outside. She could feel his toes clinging to her as he balanced himself. He wrapped his arms around her head for good measure. She laughed.

Andy and Rufus were sitting on the front stoop.

"Want to go to the beach?" she asked.

"Uh-uh," said Andy, shaking his head. "Me and Rufus are going collecting."

"Suit yourself," said Celie, maneuvering past the wagon, which was parked in the middle of the sidewalk.

There was a crowd of kids in front of the Cupboard. Ben was there with his girlfriend, Julie Thompson.

"Well, looka there. A monkey!" Pauly McCabe said as Celie got near.

All of a sudden Ben's whole gang was standing around Celie and Charley. Ben was scowling. He hated when his family drew attention to itself. Ma said that's what happens when you get to be a teenager. Celie thought if that was so, she'd just as soon not become one.

"My dad brought him home," Ben said, rolling his eyes in disgust. "You know how he is."

"Aw, Ben," said Julie, "he's such a sweet little thing." She smiled broadly as she stuck her hand out to pet him, and her white teeth glistened. Celie felt Charley's muscles tense. Before she could stop him, he lunged at Julie and bit her right on the finger. Julie shrieked.

Ben pushed Celie out of the way and took Julie's hand. Frowning, he examined her finger. "We'd better get it cleaned up," he said. He glared at Celie. "I'll deal with you later." Celie wasn't sure whether he meant her or Charley. But she didn't care. Ben wasn't the boss. Besides, it wasn't Charley's fault. Everyone knows you don't stick your hand in a strange animal's face.

Ben put his arm protectively around Julie and led her inside the Cupboard. Celie tied Charley outside and followed them in. It was enough to make you gag, Celie thought. The way Ben was fussing, you'd think Julie'd been attacked by a shark.

"I'm awful sorry, Julie," Celie said as Mrs. Marilla, who ran the shop, dabbed at the tooth marks on Julie's finger with Mercurochrome. It left an orange stain on her white skin. Where Charley's teeth had sunk in, there was a deeper red.

"Stupid monkey," said Ben. "When Ma finds out about this . . ."

He didn't finish the thought, but Celie knew what he meant. And she also knew he was right. "Please don't tell Ma," she said. "He won't do it again. Besides, he must have thought she was going to hurt him or something."

Julie stepped between them. She hated it when people fought. Ma said it was because her parents were at each other all the time. Julie always said she couldn't wait to get married so she could escape from home.

Sometimes Celie thought Ben clung to Julie because he figured if he held on tight, she wouldn't run off with some other guy. Julie's brother was in the army, and he was always bringing soldiers home with him on leave. Celie could tell it made Ben nervous. And Ma, too. Julie worried Ma almost as much as the war did, Celie knew. Ma didn't want Ben running off and getting married any more than she wanted him going to war. Celie had heard Ma tell Papa that she was afraid Ben would marry Julie just to keep her from marrying someone else. "It's this war," Ma said. "Everyone wants to hold on to something to keep their world from flying apart." That was just how Celie felt about Charley.

"I'm fine, really, Ben," Julie said, holding out her finger. "See? Hardly even broke the skin. Just drop it, okay? Let's go swimming."

"Yeah, Ben," said Pauly McCabe. "Let's go."

"Okay," Ben said grudgingly.

"Thanks, Julie," Celie said. Ben sure wouldn't have dropped it just because his sister wanted him to.

"Come on, Charley." Celie untied him and hoisted him back up onto her shoulder. "We know when we're not wanted, don't we?"

Charley muttered as though agreeing and dug his fingers into her hair.

"Ow!" Celie said. "Watch it!"

Charley released his grip on her hair and put his arms around her head instead.

"Thank you," Celie said. "What shall we do now, boy?"

Charley didn't answer.

"We could go to the cove or to the drawbridge to watch the boats go through. Or we could go to the library and look for books about monkeys. But what would I do with you? Miss Hastings certainly wouldn't let you in."

She decided to go to the cove and look through the tide pools since it was low tide. She went over the hill and was headed down the road past Mrs. Bentley's house when she saw a strange car parked out front. She was just thinking how odd that was—Mrs. Bentley never had visitors—when a boy came running out of the house. He was about her age but at least a head taller and thin, with close-cropped dark hair and freckles. A pair of gold wire-rimmed glasses was perched on his long, narrow nose, and when he smiled he displayed a mouthful of metal that flashed in the sun. She wondered how he'd kept the Junior Commandos away from his mouth. Imagine what the war department could do with those braces!

"Wow," he said. "Is that a real monkey?"

"What does it look like?" Celie said, trying not to stare at his teeth.

"Wow," he said again, reaching out to pat Charley. "Can I touch him?"

"He bites," Celie said, hoping that would scare him off. "And he doesn't like strangers."

"Oh," said the boy, pulling his hand away and taking a step backward. "By the way, I'm Joey Bentley."

"Bentley?" Celie said. "Are you related to Mrs. Bentley?"

"Yeah," said Joey. "She's my grandmother."

"Your grandmother?" Celie said. She didn't know Mrs. Bentley had children, let alone grandchildren.

"She's my father's mother," he said. He didn't seem to think it was strange at all. "I've never met her before, though. She and my father don't get along."

"How come?" asked Celie.

"Because he married my mother. My grandparents didn't approve."

"Why not?" Celie asked. This was just like the movies.

"Ma's Catholic."

"Oh," Celie said. She supposed that sounded like Mrs. Bentley. But then the old bat didn't approve of non-Catholics either, as far as Celie could tell.

"You live around here?" Joey said.

"Mmm. Next door." She raised her chin in the direction of the house.

Joey's braces flashed and his eyes widened. "Wow," he said. "We're neighbors."

"Neighbors?" Celie said. "But—"

"I'm going to be living here for the summer," Joey said. "My dad's in the navy and Mom's going to trade school. She's going to be a mechanic in one of the local shops for the duration. She didn't want me to be home alone all day, so they wrote to Grandma and asked if I could stay here. They were both kind of surprised when Grandma said yes."

"I'll bet," said Celie. She was kind of surprised herself.

"So is this *your* monkey?" he asked.

"Of course it's my monkey." Whose did he think it was? Sometimes boys said the dumbest things.

"Do you mind if I walk with you?" Joey asked.

Celie shrugged. "Suit yourself," she said. "But shouldn't you tell Mrs. Bentley where you're going?"

"Nah," he said. "She and Mom are talking. I think they'd rather I didn't interrupt. What's your name anyway?"

"Celie Marsh," she said.

"Can I hold the leash?"

Celie shrugged again. "I guess." He was sure full of questions. He might be a bigger pest than Andy.

"Where we going?" Joey asked, taking the leash from her hand.

"I don't know," Celie said. "The cove, I guess."

"The cove?"

"You're not from around here, are you?" Celie said.

Joey shook his head. "Boston."

Celie nodded. Boston was about an hour south. Imagine being so close and never meeting your own grandmother. Celie'd never met any of her grandparents either, but they'd all died before she was born.

They hadn't gone more than a block before Charley must have seen something, because he pulled the leash right out of Joey's hands and was up a tree and away, swinging from branch to branch, in a matter of seconds. Celie and Joey ran down the sidewalk calling him, but he was having too much fun to stop.

"Look at him go!" said Joey.

"You don't have to sound so pleased about it," Celie snapped. But it was something—the way it must have been when he was in the wild.

He was moving along at a pretty good clip and was in mid-swing when he suddenly stopped, his arms and legs going forward and his middle, where the belt was, staying behind. It reminded Celie of a cartoon. He hung for a moment in midair, then dropped straight down, squealing in surprise.

She and Joey caught up to him at last.

"What happened?" Joey said.

"His chain got tangled. See?" She pointed up into the tree where, about two feet above Charley's head, the leash was caught fast between two branches.

"Jeepers," said Joey.

"You'll have to climb up and free him," Celie said, though with Joey's scrawny arms and his slippery brown shoes, he didn't look as if he'd be able to rescue anything. Still, she wasn't going to climb that tree herself, not in her dirndl skirt with a strange boy standing underneath. She wished she'd worn dungarees.

"Me?" Joey said. "I've never climbed a tree before."

"Never too late to start," Celie said, nudging him toward the tree.

Charley had scrambled up onto a branch and was looking dolefully down at them. "Waaa, waaa, waaa," he cried.

"It's okay, Charley," Celie said. "Joey's coming to get you." She stuck the end of her braid in her mouth and chewed anxiously.

Joey wiped his palms on the sides of his pants. He walked slowly around the tree, testing the lower branches for height and heft. Finally he grabbed hold of a branch and swung his legs up and over, maneuvering himself around so he was sitting on the branch. Then he started to climb. Charley was a good halfway up the tree. As he climbed, Joey kept looking up at Charley and then down at Celie. She was afraid he'd get dizzy.

"Don't look down," Celie shouted.

"What?" Joey shouted back. He'd been reaching for the next branch just as she called to him. He took his eye off it to look at her, and he missed the branch.

Celie held her breath as he toppled forward, seemingly in slow motion. She lost sight of him for a moment through the leaves, but she heard a rustling in the branches and a snap. There was a flurry of leaves, then silence.

Celie was trying to figure out where in the tree Joey was when Jimmy DaSilva pulled up in his old pickup truck. He must have finished setting traps for the morning and been on his way home. He started around five o'clock most days.

Jimmy walked over to the tree and looked at where Celie had been staring, trying to see whether Joey was dead or alive. "What's up?" he asked.

"My monkey," she said, "and Joey."

"Oh brother," Jimmy said. "Monkey, huh?" He didn't seem particularly surprised.

In no time Jimmy had climbed the tree and lifted Joey down one-handed. That's how strong Jimmy was, and how scrawny Joey was. Then he climbed up to where Charley was perched. "Hey, big fella," he said. He spoke gently and moved slowly as he reached up and wrenched the chain free. He put Charley on his back, then climbed down. He passed the monkey to Celie and brushed off his hands, sticking one out to Joey. "Nice to meet you, Joey," he said. "You new around here?"

Joey nodded. There were a couple of scratches on his

cheeks that were oozing blood like a string of tiny red pearls. Celie could tell he was trying not to stare at Jimmy's hand where the fingers were missing.

"He's Mrs. Bentley's grandson," Celie said.

"Really?" Jimmy said.

"He's going to be staying with her for the summer."

"Yeah?" Jimmy said. "Well, I'll give you a word of warning. Stay away from this girl. She's nothing but trouble." He tugged on Celie's braid, and she felt her ears turn red.

"Says you," she said, sticking out her tongue. Jimmy got back into his truck and drove away laughing.

"What do you want to do now?" Joey asked.

Celie couldn't believe it. Hadn't he done enough letting Charley get away? "I think you'd better go home and have Mrs. B. clean up those scratches," she said. "Besides, they're probably wondering where you are."

"Want to come over?" Joey asked.

"No," Celie said, a bit more harshly than she meant to. The last thing she wanted to do was go into Mrs. Bentley's house. And that Joey would be there made it even less appealing. "I'm going to the cove." She could picture Ma frowning at her rudeness. "Maybe later," she added, crossing her fingers. She might miss Rita, but she didn't need a boy around—especially a boy who couldn't climb a tree!

As Joey walked back toward Mrs. Bentley's, Celie watched him. She hardly knew anything about him, but already he drove her nuts. She refused to feel bad about ditching him.

"Come on, Charley," she said, swinging him up onto her shoulder. "Let's go."

The cove was deserted when she got there. Papa's boat was lying upside down near the shack where the oars and life jackets were stored. The tide was coming in, and each wave crept a little farther up the stony beach. Seagulls bobbed in the water, occasionally ducking in search of food. Charley wandered around on the rocks while Celie looked for starfish and limpets in the tide pools. After a while she sat on a rock and dangled her feet in the water. The cove just wasn't any fun alone. Besides, the greenheads were out in force.

She stood up and was about to start for home when she heard the piercing wail of the air-raid siren, starting low and growing louder, until she thought her eardrums would explode. Charley jumped nervously at first and then began running around at the end of his leash in a panic. Celie knew how he felt. She should have been used to the sirens by now, but they always turned her insides to ice.

She looked up at the sky. No planes, but that didn't mean they weren't on the way. No U-boats, either, but they could be anywhere. Home was too far. She scanned the cove for a place to hide. There were no caves that she knew of in the rocks, and the shack was locked. The only thing she could see was the boat, overturned on the sand like an empty shell.

She scooped Charley up and ran for the boat. Lifting one side, she slid under. It was cool and dark and smelled of fish. The sound of the siren was muffled slightly by the wooden planks of the boat. Celie couldn't sit up straight, so she lay on her side and held Charley close to her chest. He didn't complain. His heart was beating rapidly, and now and then she felt his whole body shudder. "It's all right, Charley," she said, wondering whether it really was. "I've got you." That's what Ma would have told Celie when she was younger. Sometimes she wished she hadn't gotten too old for comforting.

When the all-clear finally blew, Celie pushed the boat off. It rocked once or twice, then lay still in the sand. The sudden torrent of sunlight made her blink. "This wasn't the one," she told Charley. "We're safe this time."

Charley climbed up onto the gunwale of the boat. "Hey, get down," Celie said. "I've got to turn that back over so it doesn't fill up with water." But Charley didn't move.

"Okay," Celie said. She put her shoulder against the side of the boat and pushed up. Charley jumped to the ground and scampered away as the boat rolled over with a thud. Celie laughed.

"I warned you," she said. Charley shook his head and Celie swung him up onto her shoulder. The sound of the siren was still ringing in her ears. Despite the sun, she suddenly felt cold. She clamped her teeth together to stop them from chattering. She couldn't wait to get home.

5

When she walked through the front door, Celie breathed in the familiar smell of home. She needed to know that Ma was there and that nothing had changed, that she was safe. She was about to call her mother when she heard laughter coming from the kitchen. Ma wasn't alone.

"Who's here?" she whispered to Charley, who was perched on her shoulder.

Celie closed the door quietly behind her and walked softly toward the kitchen. Her mother was sitting at the table, and when Celie rounded the corner she stopped dead. Joey. She pulled back. Maybe they didn't see me, she thought. Maybe I can get up to my room before—

"Celie?" Ma called.

Shoot. "Yes?" She didn't move.

"Look who's here."

Rats. She had to go in. She swung Charley down from her shoulder and forced a smile to her face. Ma was watching her carefully. "Hi," she said through clenched teeth, trying to sound pleased to see the boy who'd almost lost her monkey.

Joey grinned. "Hi!" he said, and waved at her, bending his hand at the wrist and waggling his fingers like the feathery legs of a barnacle searching for food. He reminded her of a puppy, all eager and dopey. Later she'd have to ask Ma whether she'd known Mrs. Bentley had a grandson.

"I ran into Joey out front," Ma said. "I was asking him about the scratch on his face." She lifted an eyebrow in Celie's direction, and Celie looked at her feet. There was no keeping secrets from Ma. "The air-raid siren went off, and I told him to come in here and get under the table," Ma said.

"Ah," Celie said. She couldn't have let him go home? It wasn't as though he lived far away.

"So I guess you two have already met," Ma said.

"Mmm," said Celie. "Yup." She couldn't think of anything else to say, so she just stood there with that smile plastered on her face.

"He's going to be staying with his grandmother for the summer," Ma said.

"Yeah," said Celie, "I know."

"And you're practically the same age. Joey just turned thirteen. Isn't that nice? You'll have someone to play with."

Play with, thought Celie. Leave it to her mother to make her sound like a baby. And in front of an almost stranger, too. A *boy* stranger. Was this how Ben felt? "Mmm," she said again. "Great." Her cheeks were beginning to burn from holding the smile. On top of that, they were now hot with embarrassment.

"Why don't you go wash up and put Charley in the summer kitchen. I'll bet he's ready for a nap. Then you and Joey can have lunch and get to know each other."

"Swell," Celie said. She doubted Charley needed a nap— that was Ma's way of getting rid of him—but she was glad for the chance to get out of the kitchen and stop smiling. Ma was up to something. She was acting like a matchmaker. Celie didn't like it one bit. But that explained why she'd made Joey stay when the air-raid siren went off.

"Here you go, Charley," she said as she placed the monkey in his crate. He didn't look at all sleepy. "Ma thinks you need a nap." She tossed her braids behind her back.

Charley looked up at her with such a pitiful expression that she couldn't help laughing.

"Hey," she said, "don't look at me." She scratched his head. "At least you don't have to play with Joey Bentley all afternoon."

"Celie?" Ma stuck her head in the door. "What are you doing? Joey's waiting."

"Joey's waiting," Celie mouthed the words to Charley and grimaced. "Coming," she said, and stood up, sticking the end of her braid in her mouth.

"And get your hair out of your mouth," Ma said, swatting at it. "That's a disgusting habit."

Celie clenched her hands into fists by her sides and spit out the braid. "Yes, ma'am," she said.

Ma flashed her a look that said, Don't yes-ma'am me, and led her back to the kitchen table, where Joey was drinking a tonic.

Celie couldn't believe Ma had given him one of the few bottles of root beer in the house! You could hardly get tonic anymore with the war on. She was about to say so when she noticed Ma's warning expression and bit her tongue.

"Here," Ma said, setting two sandwiches on the table. "You two have some lunch and then you can go outside."

"Thanks, Mrs. Marsh," Joey said, smiling again. Why was he always smiling? It made Celie want to spit.

Ma and Joey talked while he and Celie ate their sandwiches. Then Joey took a last swallow from the brown bottle, and Ma cleared the table.

"Come on, Joey," Celie said, trying to sound as uninterested as she possibly could. She headed for the back door and went out onto the porch, letting the screen slap back on its spring behind her. She heard the metallic shudder of the wire mesh as it struck Joey.

"Ow," Joey said, grabbing his elbow. You'd think she'd hit him with a sledgehammer.

"Lucille," Ma said. She was in trouble. Ma called her by her full name when she'd gone too far.

"Sorry," Celie muttered, and headed down the porch steps. Joey followed. Celie had no idea what she was supposed to do with him. She doubted that he had a baseball mitt, so they couldn't play catch. "What do you want to do?" she asked, sitting down on the wall.

Joey shrugged. "I don't know," he said. "What do you want to do?"

"I don't know," Celie said. She thought she might

scream. What was her mother thinking? "You're sure you shouldn't go home? I mean to your grandmother's? Don't you need to unpack or something?"

"Nah," said Joey. "I didn't bring much with me. Some books. Some clothes."

"So what do you think of old Mrs. B.?" Celie asked. She couldn't imagine being dumped off at Mrs. Bentley's house for the summer. It was bad enough to have her baby-sit. She was glad Ma hadn't gone to work to support the war effort. That was important and all, but Celie would hate it.

"I don't know," Joey said. He shrugged. "She's okay, I guess."

Okay? Mrs. Bentley? Jeepers, this boy was weird. "So you don't mind being dumped with some grandmother you never met?"

Joey shrugged again. "There's a war on," he said. "My mom didn't want to be a mechanic, either, but she said we've all got to do what we can."

"I guess," Celie said. She was still glad *her* ma wasn't going anywhere.

They sat for a while on the wall, then Celie said, "We could go to the drawbridge and watch the boats."

"Is that the bridge we drove over when we came into town?" Joey asked.

"Yeah," said Celie. She and Rita used to spend hours down there watching the drawbridge open to let the boats go through.

"Okay," Joey said. "I probably should tell my grand-mother first. And say goodbye to my mother. She said she was leaving after lunch."

"Yeah, you go ahead and do that," Celie said, tossing her braids behind her shoulders with a shake of her head. "I'll get Charley," she added. He'd surely be ready to get out of the summer kitchen by now, and Ma would be glad to be rid of him. Maybe if they got far enough from the house, out of Ma's line of sight, she could ditch Joey and see if there was a pickup game at the ball field.

Charley jumped up and ran to her as soon as she opened the door. She swung him onto her shoulder and started through the kitchen to the front door.

"You be careful with him," Ma warned.

"I will," Celie said, and went next door to meet Joey. The strange car was gone, so Joey's mother must have left. Celie waited in the front yard for a while, hoping he'd come out. She never liked going into Mrs. Bentley's house. It had an old smell to it, like an ancient cave. It was dark and musty, and Mrs. B. was very fussy about what you could touch and where you could walk. It was as if she lived in a museum or something, except there were no great treasures there at all that Celie could see.

Finally she went up the creaky front steps and knocked on the door. There was a clacking of heels on the wooden floor that was muffled when Mrs. Bentley reached the flow-ered rug by the front door. The door squeaked open and Mrs. Bentley's pinched face peered out. She always looked suspicious when she answered the door, as though she expected to find a robber brandishing a gun.

"Hey, Mrs. B.," Celie said, remembering too late that hay was for horses.

Mrs. Bentley frowned, but she didn't say anything about hay. She was too distracted by Charley. "That's the creature that caused Joseph to fall out of the tree?" she asked, nodding in Charley's direction.

"He didn't exactly fall out of the tree," Celie said. "He slipped is all."

Mrs. Bentley grunted. "Well, don't let it happen again."

Celie was going to say that Joey was the one who let Charley get loose to begin with, but she thought better of it. "Is Joey ready?" she asked.

Mrs. Bentley grunted again and closed the door. Celie wasn't sure whether that meant Joey couldn't come or that Mrs. Bentley was going to get him, so she sat on the stoop and put Charley down. They were just minding their own business and waiting for Joey when Mrs. Bentley's cat, Muffin, started up the front walk. Charley perked up, and Celie held his leash tighter. The cat stopped and looked at Charley. Then she seemed to decide he wasn't a danger and started to walk past.

Celie was beginning to think she had worried for nothing, when Charley jerked forward and yanked the cat's tail. The cat yowled and shot up onto the porch, howling as though she'd been attacked by a bear. The front door banged open, and Mrs. Bentley came out moving faster than

Celie had ever seen her move. Her face was blotchy red; her eyes shone with rage.

"What has that beast done to my poor Muffin?" she shrieked. She picked up the cat, which looked at Celie and Charley with what Celie could have sworn was a smug expression. "Out," Mrs. Bentley croaked, pointing a shaky finger toward the road. "Get that creature out of my yard."

Mrs. Bentley held Muffin close to her chest and turned toward the door. Just as she was shutting it behind her, Joey slipped past her and onto the porch. "See you, Grandma," he said.

"Wait a minute," Mrs. Bentley called after him. "You forgot your jacket." Joey stopped on the top step and turned to face his grandmother. "You never know when it will get cold," she said. She disappeared behind the door and returned with a dopey blue cap and a tan jacket.

Joey put on the hat and tied the jacket around his waist.

"Now, you be back by suppertime," Mrs. Bentley said, wagging her finger at him. Then she shut the door firmly behind her.

What a grump, Celie thought. For someone who had never met her grandson, she wasn't working very hard at getting him to like her. But Joey didn't say anything, so Celie didn't raise the subject. She felt kind of sorry for him, though.

The drawbridge was down the street and around the corner at what everybody called the Cut, where the Annisquam River meets the harbor. Sometimes ships were too tall to get under the bridge, so the man in the control booth stopped the traffic and lifted the bridge. Today there wasn't much action, mostly the navy ships sitting in the harbor.

"My father's on a ship like that," Joey said. "Out in the Pacific."

Celie nodded. "You must miss him," she said.

Joey just shrugged, but it was the kind of shrug that said, I miss him so bad I can't stand it. Celie knew it because she had her own shrug exactly like it. She couldn't imagine Papa going off to war. Fathers at war sometimes didn't come back. Navy ships, big as they were, sometimes sank. But Papa said he couldn't go because of his bad ear.

She thought about Ben then. In another year, Ben could go. He wanted to. He had friends who'd faked their papers and joined up even though they weren't really old enough. Ma said if he wanted to get killed that bad, she'd save him the trouble of enlisting. She didn't really mean it, but it stopped Ben from talking about it most of the time—in front of Ma, anyway.

Celie picked up Charley and put him on the railing. Then she leaned on her elbows next to him and looked out over the harbor.

She and Rita used to spend long summer hours in the shadow of the Fisherman's Memorial statue watching the boats. They would see one coming and they'd bet on whether it would be able to get through the canal without the drawbridge going up. It was a real science, because a lot depended on the tide.

"Look at that one," she said to Joey. "The bridge'll have to go up for it."

"I guess so," Joey agreed.

Celie sighed. He wasn't supposed to agree with her. How could they bet? She watched as the trawler approached the bridge. It was moving slowly, maneuvering its way directly in front of the bridge. Celie was beginning to think maybe she was wrong when she heard the toot of the ship's horn and the bridge bells began to ring, warning drivers that the gates were going to swing shut and block the traffic on the road over the bridge.

"Ha!" Celie said. "I told you!"

"Yeah," said Joey. "You were right."

It was hopeless, Celie thought. The game just wasn't fun without a loser. A breeze off the water raised goose bumps on her arms and she shivered. She was beginning to wish Mrs. Bentley had made *her* bring a jacket.

She watched as a seagull cracked a crab on the rocks below, smashing it against the seaweed-bearded granite. Lobstermen were pulling up traps. A boy and his father were casting for sea bass.

"Well, what do you want to do now?" she asked.

"I don't mind watching the boats a while longer."

"But, Joey, there are hardly any boats to watch today."

"I don't mind," Joey said again.

"Well, I mind," said Celie. "How about we go to the library? You need to get a library card if you're going to be here all summer."

"I guess," he said.

"Of course you do," Celie said. "Everybody needs a library card."

6

When they got to the library, Celie tied Charley to a small tree. "You be good," she told him. "We'll be right back."

Charley squatted down on his haunches and blinked up at her as though being naughty was something that had never crossed his mind.

"You sure he'll be all right out here alone?" Joey asked.

"Sure I'm sure," Celie said, as though she left him alone outside the library all the time. "He's only a monkey. What could he do?"

Celie loved the library. It was an old Victorian mansion. The children's room was around back. They walked up the wooden stairs to the second floor. Inside, the librarian sat at a large oak desk. Books lined every wall. The musty smell of old books mixed with the sweet scent from the new ones. Celie could see why Miss Hastings, the librarian, always had the hint of a smile on her face.

There was nothing in the card catalog about rhesus monkeys, but Miss Hastings showed them where to find the books on mammals, and Celie found some information about monkeys in the index of one.

"Joey needs a library card," Celie told Miss Hastings. "He's staying with his grandmother this summer."

"I see," said Miss Hastings. She handed Joey an application. "Fill this out and your card will be ready the next time you come in," she said.

Joey picked up a pencil and began to write. He stuck his tongue out the side of his mouth and pressed down so hard on the pencil that Celie was sure the tip would break.

"If you want a book today, I could take it out for you," Celie said.

"Thanks," said Joey. "Do you have Arthur Ransome's Swallows and Amazons books?" he asked Miss Hastings.

Miss Hastings beamed. You'd think she'd just been handed the key to a new house. "Why yes, Joseph," she said. "They're right over here. Which one are you up to?"

"I just finished *Winter Holiday*," Joey said.

"Oh, then you'll need *Coot Club*," Miss Hastings said, reaching up and pulling it off the shelf. "How about you, Lucille?" she asked, turning to Celie. "Do you need something to read besides that mammal book?"

Celie blushed. She didn't want to admit in front of Joey that lately all she'd read was the Bobbsey Twins, which she was really too old for. She hadn't read any of the Swallows and Amazons books. "I guess I'll take the first one in the series," she said. "I've been meaning to get to it," she added, crossing her fingers behind her back. Why hadn't Miss Hastings ever told her about these books if they were so great?

Miss Hastings pulled *Swallows and Amazons* off the shelf and handed it to Celie. "Good choice," she said.

They followed Miss Hastings back to the desk. There she stamped the due date on the card in the pocket at the back of each book.

"Come on, Joey," Celie said as she picked up the last of her books. "Charley's probably getting lonely."

She was just about to explain to Miss Hastings that Charley was the reason she needed books about monkeys when she heard a loud shriek from outside.

At first Celie thought the shriek had come from Charley, but when they got outside, she saw a boy about Andy's age standing on the sidewalk bawling. Celie closed her eyes tight and tried to wish the scene away. Please don't let him be bleeding, she prayed, thinking Charley must have bitten him.

Then she ran down the steps, with Joey on her heels. When she reached the boy, she stopped short. Charley was sitting on the sidewalk, eating a vanilla ice cream cone and looking very pleased with himself. It was too much. Celie sat down on the grass in front of the library and started to laugh, and Joey joined her.

"Hey, it's not funny," said the boy, whose face was streaked with ice cream and tears. The way he said it, it sounded like "snot funny," which made Celie laugh even harder. Before long, she and Joey were rolling in the grass, laughing so hard they were crying.

"I'm going to tell the library lady on you," the boy said.

Celie stopped laughing. All she needed was to have Miss Hastings call her mother. "Look," she said, "I'm sorry about your ice cream." She tried to sound sympathetic. "What happened, anyway?"

"I was walking down the street, and I saw this monkey," the boy said, wiping his nose with the back of his hand and sniffing loudly. "I came up close so I could see him better, and he jumped up and made me drop my ice cream. And he took it!" he wailed.

"What'll I do?" Celie said to Joey. "I don't have any money to buy him a new cone. But if he tells, Ma will kill me. Not to mention what she'll do to Charley."

Joey dug into his pocket and pulled out a shiny nickel. "Here," he told the boy. "Go buy yourself another cone."

The boy grabbed the coin with his sticky hand. "I don't know if they're still open," he said. "They might not have any left." But he headed back in the direction of the ice cream shop, and Celie and Joey stayed on the grass while Charley finished his cone.

"Thanks," Celie said. "Where'd you get a nickel?"

"My mother gave me money for emergencies," Joey said. "I guess that qualified."

"That was awful nice of you," Celie said. She wasn't sure she would have done the same for him.

Joey shrugged and his ears turned red. "That's okay," he said. "What are friends for?"

"Yeah," she said, trying to be polite. "Right." But Celie wished he hadn't put it that way. She didn't think of him as a friend, but now she felt as though she owed him. How could you not be nice to someone who got you out of a fix?

"We'd better get going," she said, unhitching Charley and swinging him up onto her shoulder. Maybe she could get a snack, then unload Joey and go to the park. She didn't want the guys at the ball field to see her with Joey the Jinx. That's what he was, she thought. A jinx. Whenever he was around, something bad happened. "Mrs. Bentley is probably wondering where you went to," she said hopefully.

Joey picked up the pile of books. "I don't think so. She said to be home by supper. I don't think she really wants me around," he said. "I think I remind her too much of my dad."

"But he's her own son," Celie said. "How can she not want to be reminded of him?"

Joey shrugged. "I guess when you disown a person, you don't like to remember them too much. Maybe it makes you feel bad."

"I guess," said Celie. "Well, I'm going to get something to eat and go down to the park. You can come if you want to. You got a mitt?"

Joey shook his head. "I'm not too good at sports," he said. "Mom says I have poor eye/hand coordination."

"Ah," said Celie, nodding as though she knew what he meant. Who talked like that anyway?

They walked along, past the drawbridge, which was still pretty quiet, toward home.

"I guess I'll see you later," Celie said, heading up the

driveway to her house. But Joey followed her. He was like a stray dog. Right then she wouldn't have minded a stray dog as much as she minded Joey.

Ma was outside working in the Victory Garden. She'd started it last spring and grew a lot of the food they ate all winter. There were beans and tomatoes, carrots and potatoes. And plenty of Swiss chard, because that was Papa's favorite vegetable.

"Hey, you two!" Ma called. She waved her trowel in their direction.

"Hey," Celie said.

"Hello, Mrs. Marsh," said Joey. He waved back. Celie looked down and rolled her eyes, hoping Ma wouldn't notice.

"Hungry?" Ma asked. "I made cookies."

Cookies? Celie couldn't remember the last time Ma had made cookies.

"Sure, Ma," she said, stifling a groan. She'd never be able to ditch Joey now.

"I'd love some," said Joey.

"Go wash up," Ma said. "I'll pour the milk."

Celie went into the house with Joey. She put Charley down and went to the kitchen sink, where she rubbed her hands together under the tap, then wiped them on the dish towel. Joey turned on the hot water and waited until it was steamy. He took up the bar of soap and worked it into a lather, then ran his soapy hands under the faucet until they were pink from the heat. He dried them on the towel, carefully avoiding the area where Celie had left damp brown smudges. Jeepers, Celie thought, he was just too perfect. No wonder grownups liked him!

★

Ma wouldn't let them go to the park right away. "You have to digest," she said.

"But, Ma—" Celie started to protest.

"No *buts*," Ma said.

So Celie put her books into the basket she kept on a rope by the tree house to lift supplies in. Joey put his book on top.

"You go on and pull the basket up," she told Joey.

Joey carefully climbed the rope ladder. He held on so tight that his knuckles were pure white.

When he got to the top, he clambered into the tree house and sat there a moment catching his breath. Celie watched, shaking her head. "The books, Joey," she called.

Joey nodded and crawled to where the rope hung over the edge. He reached out one hand and grabbed the rope and began to pull.

Celie waited while he emptied the basket and let it back down. She held the basket steady with her foot and carefully placed Charley inside. "You stay there, Charley," she said. The monkey looked up at her and blinked. He seemed worried.

"Okay," she called to Joey, "pull." Joey peered over the side. When he saw Charley, his mouth opened as though he were about to say something, but then he shut it and began to pull. With the first tug, the basket swung and Charley leaped out.

"Charley!" Celie called, but he took off up the tree and

didn't look back until he was safely on the tree house floor. Celie laughed. "Well, that's one way to get you up there," she said, and scampered up the ladder after him.

Celie wasn't happy about sharing her tree house with a boy, but she didn't figure she had any choice, since Ma was on Joey's side. She hooked Charley's leash to a branch and opened the book about mammals. There was a picture of two monkeys picking at each other's fur. The caption said they were looking for parasites.

"Yuck," said Celie. She quickly turned the page.

"What's wrong?" Joey said. "That's how they stay clean. It's natural."

"Still," said Celie, "I don't like to think about parasites."

There were mother monkeys feeding baby monkeys, father monkeys ferociously defending their territory, and brother and sister monkeys playing tag through the treetops. There was a picture of a mother standing in front of her baby, her long canine teeth flashing like sabers, her eyes black with fury. Celie thought she wouldn't like to be whatever predator was facing that angry mother.

"Neat," said Joey, looking over Celie's shoulder.

"Yeah," said Celie. "They are."

She was reading something about how rhesus monkeys get more aggressive as they reach adolescence and wondering how old Charley was when she looked over and saw him picking at his fur, just like the monkey on the parasite page. "Ew," she said. "Charley, you'd better not have bugs." Charley put whatever it was he'd picked out of his fur into his mouth.